A Witch
Called Rosa

A Witch
Called Rosa

Hilary Hawkes

First edition published by Robinswood Press 2005.

© Hilary Hawkes 2005.

Cover and internal illustrations © Caroline Crossland 2005.

Design and layout by Lorraine Payne.
Printed by Latimer Trend Ltd, Plymouth.

Robinswood Press

Stourbridge England
Dublin Republic of Ireland

ISBN 1-869981-820

A Witch
Called Rosa

Hilary Hawkes

Illustrated by
Caroline Crossland

Hilary Hawkes Books

About the Author

Hilary Hawkes grew up in Fareham, Hampshire. She loved listening to stories and started to write her own at the age of eight. By the time she was sixteen, Hilary had already written two novels of 70,000 words each! But she couldn't find anyone to publish them yet. She persevered and, when she reached nineteen, Hilary "got lucky" – a magazine recognised her as a brilliant storyteller and, at last, dozens of her newest short stories were published.

Hilary took a degree in English and Publishing, and started work as an editorial assistant. Later, as a mother of three, she discovered the joys of assisting in a nursery class – subsequently training as a Montessori teacher – and began to write stories again. Two of these – *125, Go!* and *There's a grandad in my soup!* – were published by Scripture Union Publishing and a number of contributions by Hilary have been included in books published by Learning Development Aids (LDA).

She now lives in Oxfordshire with her husband, Peter, and sons David, Richard and Matthew. In between teaching, being Mum-the-Taxi-driver, walking Hattie the dog and doing things like mending the ceiling where the electrician fell through, she's thinking up lots more stories for us all...

Inspired by Matthew.

Chapter One

Charlie was in a hurry. He crashed down the stairs two at a time.

Polly had said, "Bet you can't get some food from the kitchen and get back up here in thirty seconds!"

And Charlie had said, "Bet I can!"

He leapt towards the kitchen door. The sticker on it said:

Charlie didn't knock. His mum was sitting on the kitchen table yacking down the phone. She was wearing a pair of Dad's old trousers and one of Dad's really old shirts. They were covered in paint and blobs of wallpaper paste.

Charlie grabbed open the nearest food cupboard. A giant bag of twenty-four packets of assorted crisps fell out.

He peered further back.

"There's nothing decent," he said.

His mum stopped yacking down the phone. She pointed at an unopened packet of chocolate biscuits.

"Take those," she said. "I want to get that lounge wall finished before I start the tea."

Mum was always redecorating bits of the house. Charlie huffed. There were only ten seconds left to win the challenge. He took the biscuits and rocket-sped straight back up to his sister's room.

"Twenty-eight!" said Polly as he skid-stopped in front of the window.

"I won!" said Charlie. He tore open the biscuit packet. "Have I missed much?"

Charlie and Polly lived at number 42 Bellway Street. They had been staring out of Polly's bedroom window for ages. They were watching the new neighbours at number 44.

Two furniture shop delivery men were carrying a new wardrobe up to the neighbours' front door. They wobbled and staggered. There was a lot of shouting going on.

"What are they saying?" Polly said.

Charlie opened the window.

"I SAID IT'S NEVER GOING THROUGH THAT DOOR!" one of the men was yelling.

The new neighbours, a woman, a man, a little girl and an old woman, were watching. Charlie thought the girl looked about ten – like him. Polly thought she looked about nine – like her. The old woman was waving her arms around.

"Watch what you're doing. Don't bash anything!"

The delivery men wobbled to a halt.

"Oh, just put it down! Put it down!" the old woman shouted.

Charlie and Polly thought the delivery men were right. There was no way that giant wardrobe was going to fit through that front door. The men went back to the van.

"If you want something done properly, do it yourself," the old woman said.

She walked over to the wardrobe. To Charlie's and Polly's amazement she started pushing it quickly up the path to the front door.

Then the weirdest thing happened. The giant cupboard seemed to lift itself up. It floated through the doorway.

Polly's eyes nearly popped out of their sockets.

"How did that happen? It did look too big to go through the door!"

Charlie frowned. What a wicked trick!

"I wish we could get to meet them," he said. "It's been nearly a week since they moved in."

It was true. Charlie and Polly and their mum and dad had called round three times to say hello to the new neighbours. Mum said it was a polite thing to do. But the new neighbours always seemed to be out. Or maybe they just didn't answer the door. Mum said she had heard some strange noises when she had rung the doorbell. It was a sort of snorting, snuffling noise. Another time, when Charlie had been looking out of an upstairs window, he thought he had seen a large pink pig in the neighbours' garden! But Polly hadn't believed him.

The delivery men wasted no time getting away.

"Let's get out of here. They're nuts, this family. Did you see that old woman? Spooky. It's not normal."

Suddenly there was a squeaky, squealy sound. Something small and pink scuttled out of the neighbours' house. The girl ran forward to catch it.

"No you don't, Chipolata!" she said. She scooped up a piglet.

Polly gasped.

"There you are!" said Charlie. "I told you they had a pig! I thought it was bigger than that though. Maybe they've got lots of them."

"Ughh!" said Polly.

That evening, Charlie told their parents about the wardrobe and the pig. Dad said the old lady might be a secret Heavy-Weights-Lifting-Champion or something. Mum said the pig sounded like a health hazard. Charlie wanted to ask if they could try going round again to say hello. Then Mum started talking about her evening class.

Mum went to evening classes in Decorating and Home Design. She came home with all sorts of wacky ideas like knitted curtains.

"Next week we're doing green ceilings," said Mum.

"Oh dear," said Dad.

"I need to take some samples of different shades of green," said Mum.

"And are you... er... thinking of trying them out on the sitting room ceiling?" said Dad nervously.

"Oh, no!" said Mum.

"Good!" said Dad.

"I'm waiting until I've been to the purple ceiling class before I decide which would look best."

Later, Charlie was sent to bed at his usual time – eight-thirty. A bit of careful nagging extended this to nine o'clock. When he was just about to get into bed, he heard voices coming from the new neighbours' back garden. He peeped through the gap in the curtains.

The neighbours were all standing in the garden in the dark. But the real nutcase bit was what two of them were doing. The two women had a vacuum cleaner each.

Were they about to vacuum the garden? Charlie laughed out loud. Then he gasped. Suddenly he felt extremely light-headed and wobbly around the knees – the way you feel when you've just seen something that can't possibly happen.

Perched on the vacuum cleaners, the two women seemed to be lifting gently off the ground and gliding slowly up into the night sky! And they were each holding – a pig!

"See you later, honeys!" they called down to the man and little girl. "Don't stay up too late, Rosa."

Charlie's heart was pounding so hard it hurt. His knees gave way and he fell in a heap in front of the window.

Chapter Two

There was no way Charlie was going to sleep after that. He crashed into Polly's room. Polly was already snoring loudly. He prodded her until she was awake. Then he told her what he had seen.

"You're making it up!" Polly said grumpily. She hadn't wanted to be woken up.

"Of course I'm not making it up!"

"Maybe you dreamt it!"

Charlie was annoyed.

"I didn't dream it. If I'd dreamt it then I'd have been in bed asleep. I was wide awake, standing by the window."

Polly groaned. She didn't believe Charlie. It sounded too daft.

That was it. Charlie had had enough. If Polly didn't believe him then there was nothing else for it. The next day he would have to meet the neighbours and confront them about the whole thing. And Polly would have to come with him.

The next morning Charlie rang the doorbell to

number 44. Polly stood next to him, arms folded. She couldn't believe that her brother was still going on about the flying vacuum cleaner nonsense.

They almost jumped when someone pulled back the heavy front door. The young girl was standing there. She smiled at Charlie and Polly.

"Hi!"

"Hi!" said Charlie, feeling nervous. "I'm Charlie and this is Polly. We live next door. We came round to..."

"To say... hello," said Polly. She really didn't want her brother saying anything about flying vacuum cleaners yet.

"Hello, I'm Rosa," said the girl. "Do you want to come in?"

This was an invitation Charlie couldn't resist. They followed Rosa. They had never been inside number 44 before. The hallway was long and dark. Charlie's foot got tangled in something. He fell headlong over a hard object that had been left in the way. Then, before he could stop her, Polly had fallen on top of him. They both ended up in a hopeless heap.

"Ouch! What did you do that for?"

"I didn't do anything. I couldn't see!"

Someone flicked a light switch. Charlie and Polly looked to see what they had fallen over.

Vacuum cleaners! Two of them!

"See!" hissed Charlie.

Polly rubbed her leg.

"It proves nothing!" she whispered.

Charlie suddenly realised that the grown-ups in Rosa's family were staring at them.

One rushed to help them to their feet. It was Rosa's mum, Mrs Bollygum.

The other two were Rosa's dad, Mr Bollygum, and Rosa's grandmother, whom they called Gran. Gran was standing in front of a shut door. Charlie had just seen her shut it firmly as if she didn't want them seeing inside. Very odd, thought Charlie, and he wondered what they got up to in there.

"Come in to the kitchen," said Gran. "I was just going to put the kettle on."

Mr Bollygum was just leaving for work.

"I have a lorry full of frozen sausages to drive right down to Cornwall. I might be late home."

A high-pitched squeak came from the kitchen.

"It's all right, Chipolata," said Rosa. "He's not talking about you."

"Are you really going to drive all the way to Cornwall?" Charlie asked Mr Bollygum.

"Well, I won't get there any other way!"

Hmmm. Really? Charlie thought. He wanted to ask if it was faster by vacuum cleaner. He thought Mrs Bollygum and Gran were giving each other funny looks.

As they walked into the kitchen, Rosa picked up a small, clean pig.

"You don't mind pigs, do you?" said Rosa.

"I don't think so," said Polly. "I've never met any before. Why have you got them?"

"They're just pets," Mrs Bollygum said quickly. She

pointed at the kitchen table and chairs.

"Do sit down."

Just then two larger pigs trotted into the kitchen from the hallway. They sat down in a basket by the back door. Polly's mouth dropped open. Charlie laughed.

"These two are called Prince and Posh," said Mrs Bollygum.

"Did you get them the same time as the vacuum cleaners?" asked Charlie. Polly kicked him under the table.

Charlie thought he saw Mrs Bollygum and Gran give each other strange looks again. But Rosa was talking. Rosa sounded really nice. She was nine like Polly. A school holiday had just started and, when it was over, Rosa would be going to the same school as Charlie and Polly. She would be in Polly's class.

"Charlie's got something really daft to ask you," Polly said. "He had a weird dream – but he thinks it's real."

"Well, thanks a lot," Charlie said, crossly. "I told you it wasn't a dream. It was real."

"What was real?" Rosa said. She had sat down at the kitchen table with Chipolata on her lap.

Polly was starting to giggle. "You're not going to believe this, but..."

"Shut up, Polly!" Charlie said.

But Polly couldn't shut up. "Charlie thinks you've got... got... have got..."

"Have got what? What's so funny?" asked Rosa.

"Flying vacuum cleaners!" Polly giggled.

Charlie was furious. This was no laughing matter. He had seen it with his own eyes. It was real. Not imagined. Not funny. He could tell by the look on Rosa's face that it wasn't funny.

There was a long silence. Now Rosa was doing the strange looks.

Polly stopped laughing.

"There," said Charlie, "I told you there was something to this."

Gran was whispering to Mrs Bollygum.

"How could he have seen us?" she hissed. "It was dark."

"If only we hadn't missed that bus," said Mrs Bollygum. "It's going to be just like the last place we lived. And we haven't been here five minutes yet."

"Sneaky neighbours spying on us," Gran said.

Mrs Bollygum looked at Charlie and Polly. She

stared long and hard at them and then she smiled. She turned back to Gran.

"They're just innocent children," she said. "But clever ones. It's not their fault they're so nosy. As long as we make sure no one else finds out. Rosa, you'd better explain it to them."

By now the kettle was boiling and Mrs Bollygum was asking who wanted hot chocolate.

"Now listen," Rosa said. "There's no easy way to say this."

Mrs Bollygum shovelled spoonfuls of chocolate in to three mugs.

"What you saw last night, Charlie, was... well, it was real."

Mrs Bollygum didn't appear to have lifted the kettle, but it was pouring hot water into the mugs all by itself.

Mrs Bollygum dropped a spoonful of sugar into each cup. She wasn't touching the spoons, but they seemed to be stirring by themselves.

Charlie's eyes darted from Rosa to the mugs.

"You see," Rosa was still speaking, "Mum, Gran and I are... well, we're... "

The mugs rose slowly off the kitchen surface all by

themselves and swayed their way across to the kitchen table. Charlie and Polly looked in disbelief as the drinks landed – one in front of Rosa, one in front of Polly and one spilling slightly in front of Charlie.

"… we're witches." Rosa finished.

"And gone are the days of witches on broomsticks with black cats," Gran said. "These days it's vacuum cleaners and whatever pets you happen to have. Can't remember when I last saw a good broomstick."

There was a long silence.

If Charlie hadn't been sitting down, his knees would definitely have been wobbling.

Rosa's mum was looking at the mugs as though everything was quite normal.

"Anyone for a biscuit?" she said.

Chapter Three

Charlie decided this was the weirdest weekend ever.

The Bollygums were witches? They were living next door to a family of witches? Mr Bollygum wasn't one, of course. Mr Bollygum was a long distance lorry driver. He drove frozen sausages to Cornwall every weekend.

Charlie and Polly had to hands-on-heart-and-hope-to-die promise that they would never tell a soul. They promised.

"People don't understand about witches, dears," Gran said. "They think they're dangerous. They think they're always doing funny spells."

"Letin lupin licky lolls," Rosa's mum said as soon as they had finished the mugs of hot chocolate.

Suddenly the breakfast bowls and plates that had been sitting innocently in the washing-up bowl started jerking and turning and bashing into each other.

"No! No!" Mrs Bollygum shrieked.

"That's not meant to happen!" Rosa said.

"I know that! I know that!" said Mrs Bollygum.

Rosa looked at Charlie and Polly.

"It's Mum's Washing-up Instruction," she said. "It doesn't always work though."

"Letin lupin licky lolls!" Mrs Bollygum tried again.

This time the taps started filling the bowl with water, the washing-up liquid bulls-eyed a few drops of itself onto the plates and a small brush started scrubbing and rubbing at the crockery.

"That's more like it," Mrs Bollygum sighed. She looked at the children.

"It's not easy being a witch, you know," she said. "It takes days... months... *years* of practice to get an Instruction right. Rosa will tell you. She hasn't even done her first Instruction yet."

"Wow!" said Charlie. "That's terrible."

It seemed this was true. Rosa explained that, by the age of eight, most young witches would be expected to have mastered their first Instruction – or Spell as they were called in Gran's day. But Rosa couldn't. Rosa couldn't even fly her own vacuum cleaner yet.

"The Annual Witches' Meeting is only a week away," her mum said. "It doesn't look as if you'll be able to take part this year, either."

Rosa was looking annoyed. Only witches who could fly and had mastered their first Instruction could attend the Annual Witches' Meeting.

"You don't practise enough," Gran was saying. "When I was your age I used to practise for three hours a day."

Rosa's mum was talking spell language again.

"Pepin pupin picky polls!"

A box of saucepans, still packed from house moving, suddenly burst open. Then, colliding and crashing, the pots crammed themselves on to the top shelf of a cupboard.

"Not all on one shelf!" Mrs Bollygum shouted. "It's not strong enough!"

She was right. The shelf tipped under the weight of the saucepans and they crashed and rolled down on to the floor.

Chipolata squealed in alarm.

"Can you stay and play for a bit?" said Rosa.

"Yes, please," said Polly and Charlie. "Mum knows where we are."

"No going in the sitting room," said Gran. "Not until we've got it... er... sorted."

They were doing it again, Charlie thought. Rosa and her mum and Gran were giving each other funny looks. Whatever did they keep in that sitting room that they didn't want anyone to see?

"Do you want to play computer games?" asked Rosa. "I've got my own computer upstairs."

"Wow!" said Charlie.

They followed Rosa upstairs and stayed about an hour. Charlie was usually good at computer games, but today he couldn't concentrate. He wanted to know more about what it was like being a witch. He wanted to know what the Bollygums had hidden in the sitting room.

Later, when they were standing by the front door saying goodbye, Charlie suddenly got his chance.

Posh and Prince were excitedly sniffing around the children's shoes when Polly accidentally stepped backwards straight onto Chipolata's trotter. There was a terrible squeal and the little piglet shot off in alarm towards the sitting room door, pushed it open and disappeared inside. The door stayed ajar.

This time Rosa squealed in alarm. But it was too

late. Charlie had seen it. Even Polly who was busy saying things like "Oh, poor Chipolata! Sorry! I didn't see you there!" had seen it.

"Wow!" said Charlie, stepping towards the door.

He stepped inside the room and Polly and Rosa followed him.

"Gosh! Gosh!" was all that Polly managed to say.

"Wow! Wow!" was all that Charlie managed to say.

Charlie had been expecting to see a dingy old room full of secret witchy things. Polly had been expecting to see spare vacuum cleaners or maybe some gone wrong spells. But this was fantastic. They were standing on a plush red carpet. A chandelier hung from the ceiling. Velvet, silver-lined curtains draped gracefully from the windows. There were white and gold armchairs and a sofa. There were shiny polished tables and cupboards and dainty ornaments. Most fantastic of all was a huge portrait of the Queen over the fireplace.

Rosa seemed to want them out of the room as fast as possible. She grabbed Chipolata and ushered them back to the front door while their mouths were still open.

"What a posh room!" said Charlie, which was a bit

rude really, but he couldn't think of anything else.

Rosa was looking a bit flustered.

"I suppose your mum keeps it nice for visitors?" said Polly.

It seemed to be the only explanation.

The Bollygums were going to be one tricky secret to keep.

Chapter Four

Charlie and Polly knew it was going to be a problem keeping the neighbours' secret from their parents. It was Mum who was the real problem.

She would keep saying things like: "I really must get to know those new neighbours now. Rosa sounds nice. I'm so glad you've found a new friend."

"I expect they're really busy," Polly would say.

"They're not expecting you to go round. They know how busy you are with painting the lounge," Charlie would say.

"Do they really?" Mum would say, half way up the step ladder with the paintbrush in her hand. "Are they interested in decorating? Perhaps Mrs Bollygum would like to come to the evening class with me! "

Charlie knew Mum wouldn't be put off for ever, though. It wasn't that he didn't want his parents to get to know the Bollygums. It was just that they had promised to keep the witch thing a secret. And Charlie's mum was completely unable to keep secrets.

She worked part time at the doctors' surgery and if any embarrassing details about patients ever leaked out you could be sure it was Mum who caused the leak. Thanks to her, everyone in town now knew that Charlie's teacher, Mrs Cox, had three boils on her bottom. And thanks to Charlie's mum, everyone in town knew that Mr Pike, who worked in the newsagents, had a giant bogey stuck up one of his nostrils.

Charlie knew that Mum would eventually meet the new neighbours. He could only hope that, when she did, the Bollygums wouldn't do anything too crazy.

It was Saturday, a week later, when it happened. Rosa's mum and Gran were getting ready to go to the Annual Witches' Meeting the next day.

Mum had managed to get herself invited to the Bollygums' house. Well, Rosa had come round to play with Charlie and Polly several times over the holiday and the last time Mum had escorted her back. And, just to be polite, Mrs Bollygum had said, "You must come round for a chat sometime."

There was nothing else for it, Charlie decided. They would have to go with her. That way they could make sure she didn't ask any awkward questions or see anything too witchy.

Charlie and Polly were ready to go. They waited in front of the TV for Mum, who was still upstairs, wondering whether to wear her pink blouse with the orange spots or her orange jumper with the pink spots. Polly flipped through the channels with the remote. It was still too early for children's TV but, suddenly, something on the screen caught her eye. It was a news flash.

The announcer was standing in front of the Queen's Palace.

"Detectives here are investigating a very serious crime," she said. "The country's entire police force has been put on red alert after the disappearance last week of the Queen's Lounge."

Charlie and Polly gasped.

"Police are puzzled by the way the thieves have replaced Her Majesty's exotic possessions by what the chief Royal Detective has described as 'a load of old rubbish'."

The announcer turned to a scruffy-looking man next to her.

"Detective Chief Inspector Brains," she asked, "can you give us any details about what happened here?"

Detective Chief Inspector Brains looked at the camera.

"We're up against a gang of pranksters," he said. "The whole room has been stolen – carpets, fancy ceiling and all. But the thieves didn't leave the room empty. They've replaced it with a dirty carpet, some old wallpaper and some scruffy furniture."

"Any idea why they would want to do that?"

"No!" said the Detective.

The TV showed pictures of the Queen's missing Lounge. Charlie and Polly couldn't believe their eyes.

"It's... it's!" said Polly.

"It looks like the Bollygums' lounge!" said Charlie.

"It is the Bollygums' lounge!" said Polly. "What did they do?"

The TV was showing the Queen's missing white

and gold armchairs, silver-lined velvet curtains and shiny oak furniture. It was the Bollygums' lounge alright – or rather it was the Queen's Lounge in the Bollygums' house.

The announcer was speaking again.

"The Palace and the police are releasing this information today – seven days after the theft – because, so far, all their attempts at tracking down the criminals have failed. They are hoping members of the public may be able to help."

"Ready to go, you two?" It was Mum standing in the doorway. She had decided on the yellow T-shirt with the green stripes.

Polly quickly flicked off the TV. The last thing they needed was for Mum to discover the neighbours had part of the Queen's Palace in their house.

A few minutes later it was Rosa who opened the front door. Gran escorted Mum to the kitchen.

Charlie and Polly hung back. They desperately needed to speak to Rosa.

"We know about the room!" Charlie whispered. "Polly and I saw it on the TV just now. There was a news flash."

Rosa looked pale.

"Oh, no!" she said.

"I think you owe us an explanation," said Charlie.

"Mum and Gran will have panic attacks if they know it's been on the news," said Rosa. "What about your mum? Did she see it?"

"No," said Polly.

Charlie was cross.

"Explanation please, Rosa," he said. "What on earth have you witches been up to?"

Rosa opened the lounge door and the three stepped inside.

"It's all my fault!" said Rosa. "It happened last week. You know how they're always saying I don't practise Instructions enough? Well, I offered to try the 'tidy' Instruction on the lounge."

"And?"

"Well," Rosa said, "all I said was 'I bet I can get this as good as the Queen's sitting room!' Then I said the Instruction and this happened. It wouldn't be right to keep it. We've been trying to reverse the Instruction ever since, but it won't work."

Flying hoovers! Charlie reckoned this had to be just about the worst mess of things he had ever seen. No wonder they had kept the door shut. No wonder visitors were only invited into the kitchen.

Before he and Polly had the chance to say anything else, something horrendous happened. There was a sudden screech and scream and Mum, followed closely by Prince and Posh, rushed out of the kitchen. Charlie had always known that Mum wasn't keen on pigs. He hadn't realised she was that nervous of them.

As far as Mum was concerned, her only escape was the room to the right of the front door – the lounge. Before Rosa's mum and Gran or anyone else could stop her, she was inside, across the room and behind the sofa. Posh and Prince stopped at the door and went back to the kitchen. They seemed to sense it was a no-pig zone and, anyway, they had only wanted to be friendly, not frighten the visitor.

"Oh, no!" cried Gran. "I told you to keep that door shut at all times. "

"What are you doing in here?" Mrs Bollygum shrieked.

"It's okay," said Rosa. "Try to keep calm!"

Mum was standing with her mouth wide open. She gazed in disbelief at the walls, the ceiling and the furniture.

Charlie hardly dared to look at the portrait of the Queen over the fireplace.

Polly hardly dared to look at the royal blue wallpaper, high ceilings, brass doorknobs and chandelier.

Thank goodness Mum hadn't seen the news flash.

Rosa was right. The important thing was to keep calm and try to act normally.

Mum's eyes moved slowly around the room and its luxurious contents. Her mouth stayed open for a whole minute before she spoke.

"What an unusual room!" she said.

"They're patriotic!" said Charlie, hoping that would explain things a bit. "They're very patriotic, Mum. Lovely, isn't it?"

Charlie's mum stared at the Queen's portrait.

"Y... yes!" she said.

"Would you like a nice cup of tea?" Mrs Bollygum said. "I'll go and make it. Do sit down."

Mrs Bollygum hurried off to the kitchen and Mum plopped herself down on the Queen's white and gold sofa. Charlie choked. A cup of tea Bollygum style was exactly what his mum didn't need. Mrs Bollygum's mind must be in a whirl over what Rosa had done to the lounge. What was she thinking of?

They all sat carefully on the posh chairs and tried to think of normal things to talk about like the weather.

The first mug came floating towards the lounge door from the kitchen. It must have ignored Mrs Bollygum's Instruction to stay on the tray in the kitchen.

Charlie had to distract his mum from seeing it. He blurted out the first thing that came into his head.

"Look at that, Mum!" He pointed at nothing in particular on the other side of the room.

His mum looked away from the door and the approaching mug of tea.

"What?" she said.

"That crack in the wall," said Charlie. "Isn't it amazing the way that's been filled in?"

Charlie's mum couldn't see any cracks.

"Don't be rude, Charlie! This room looks strangely familiar. I can't think where I've seen one like it before. Those ornaments look very expensive."

Rosa and Gran looked pale.

Charlie laughed.

"Expensive?" he said. "That's what you're meant to think. It's just cheap rubbish really. Plastic mostly. Isn't it, Rosa?"

"Charlie! Stop being rude!" said Mum.

The second mug was following closely behind the first. They both hovered around the lounge door.

Charlie jumped quickly around to the other side of the room.

"What I really like about this room..." he said.

Mum looked at him in astonishment.

"... is that it's... it's..."

"So roomy!" Polly said.

"Yes! It's just so roomy!" agreed Rosa.

A third mug had joined the queue of cups outside the lounge door... They swayed across the room towards Charlie's mum.

"Ouch!" Charlie grabbed his left kneecap and dropped to the floor. Mum jumped up and hurried over to him.

"Whatever is the matter?"

"Just a bit of a twinge," Charlie said, as the tea mugs sailed carefully through the air behind his mum's back and landed on the table in front of the sofa where she had been sitting. He stood up. "It seems to have gone now."

What Charlie was really beginning to get was a headache. This was a nightmare. How was he going to stop his mum finding out that the Bollygums were witches?

Mum was puzzled, but went back to sit on the sofa.

"Tea! Lovely! I didn't see it arrive!" she said.

"That was the idea," Charlie mumbled to himself.

It was definitely a nightmare. There they all were sitting in the Queen's Lounge – Mum, Mrs Bollygum and Gran sipping tea and talking about decorating as though everything was perfectly normal.

"You're welcome to come and see our sitting room when it's finished," Mum twittered. "Of course, it's not as grand as this. This really is - exceptional. How did you do it in just a few days? I feel as though I'm sitting in a palace!"

There was a long silence. Then Mrs Bollygum picked up a plate of biscuits.

"Anyone for a ginger nut?" she said.

Chapter Five

"Detectives in London have made a breakthrough in the search for the Queen's Lounge."

It was early the next morning and the news boomed out from the telly in Charlie's and Polly's house.

"Turn it off!" said Polly. "Mum will hear it!"

Charlie turned the volume right down so Mum and Dad, who weren't up yet, couldn't hear. The news reader sounded excited.

"After taking apart an old desk left in the room, detectives found a tatty-looking diary. They are in the process of examining this and are confident it will give them some clues. They are confident of recovering the Queen's Lounge fairly soon."

"They must find a way to reverse that Instruction!" said Charlie.

The TV presenter was speaking again.

"The Queen is very upset about the disappearance of her favourite ornament. It's a small wooden pig. It was given to her by an Indian tribe and is said to have magical powers."

Charlie gasped.

"That's it!" he cried.

"What?" said Polly.

"A small wooden pig with magical powers. It must be next door right now. And it could be just the thing to reverse the spell!"

It might have been only seven o'clock on a Sunday morning, but the two of them rushed round to Rosa's house.

The Bollygums were already up. Rosa's mum opened the door. Rosa had told them about Polly and Charlie seeing the news flash.

"It's all on the news again!" Polly said in a panic. "You're going to be in terrible trouble soon."

The children followed Mrs Bollygum into the lounge where she and Gran and Rosa had been working on reversing the Instruction. They had been up all night trying to get the room back to normal. They were starting to panic.

"Calm down, everyone," Charlie said. "We might have the answer."

He explained about the wooden pig and its magical powers. They all started searching. It was Polly who eventually found it.

"You got us into this mess, Rosa. You get us out of it!" Gran said.

"Okay," said Rosa. She picked up the pig and then concentrated.

Everyone stood very still.

"Yetin yupin yicky yolls," said Rosa, which meant – put everything back the way it was.

Nothing happened.

"Yetin yupin yicky..."

A loud thumping on the front door interrupted Rosa's second attempt.

"I don't believe it!" said Charlie, looking out of the window. "There are two police cars outside."

"I told you! They've tracked you down!" said Polly. "What are we going to do?"

"How much bad luck can anyone get?" Gran sighed. "Charlie and Polly, you go to the door and keep them talking. We need longer to get this reversing Instruction to work."

"Just don't let them in here yet!" said Rosa's mum.

Charlie and Polly shut the lounge door firmly behind them and took their time opening the front one.

As soon as they did, a police detective charged through and fell splat on his face on the doormat.

Two police officers in uniform behind him tried not to snigger.

The detective got up.

"What did you do that for? I was just charging at the door when you opened it."

"Sorry," said Charlie. "What do you want?"

"What do we want? Are you being funny? Don't you listen to the news? Don't you recognise me? I'm Detective Chief Inspector Brains. I've been down at the Television Centre all the morning looking for the Queen's furniture."

"How did the Queen's furniture get in to the Television Centre?" Charlie said, trying to sound stupid.

"Don't be stupid! I mean I've been at the Television Centre talking about the missing furniture so that, when everyone switches on their televisions, they'll hear that it's still missing."

"Well, thank you very much, detective," said Polly. "Thanks for telling us about it. We'll look out for it."

The detective took a small book out of his jacket pocket.

"Not so fast, young lady!" he said.

He waved the book at Polly's face.

"See this?"

Polly shivered.

"The thieves left this at the Palace."

Charlie gulped.

"It's a diary!" said the detective. "It seems those thieves weren't as smart as they thought they were. You see, when you've been a detective for as long as I have, you start to get clever. I reckon this belongs to the thieves. And it's got their name and address in it!"

Charlie gulped again.

"Wow!" he said. "That's amazing! Shouldn't you go round there then?"

"Exactly!" said the detective. He turned back to the door.

"What do you mean, go round there? I am there." He waved the book at Charlie this time. "This is the address in the book!"

Then, before Polly or Charlie could say anything else, the officers charged past into the kitchen.

"It has to be here somewhere," the detective said. "You two check the back garden."

"He's not exactly the world's brainiest detective, is he?" Charlie whispered.

Some weird noises were coming from the lounge.

"I hope not," said Polly. "What are we going to do if the Bollygums haven't reversed the spell, Charlie?"

"Run?"

Some more weird noises came from the lounge. There were rumbles and bangs and a loud popping sound.

The detective and the two police officers had finished searching and were back in the hall approaching the lounge door.

"Just one more room," said the detective. "It must be in here."

Charlie jumped in front of the lounge door.

"I wouldn't go in there," he said. "I mean – it's a real mess."

The detective pushed Charlie out of the way and opened the door.

Charlie just couldn't look. He squeezed shut his eyes and put his fingers in his ears.

Suddenly, a ringing sound came from the Chief Detective's jacket pocket. The detective pushed back the lounge door and pulled out a mobile phone at the same time...

Chapter Six

"What a relief!" the detective shouted. "The Queen's Lounge has been found!"

Charlie was still too shocked to open his eyes. Well, he supposed it was unavoidable. He and Polly had tried really hard to stop them opening the door, but...

"Charlie!" Polly whispered. "It's okay! He's only talking on the *phone*. Look... it's gone!"

Charlie opened his eyes. Polly was right! It was gone! Gone! The Queen's Lounge had gone! The Bollygums must have managed to reverse the spell at the last second. The pig had worked!

The detective was speaking into his phone and was walking back to the front door. "You mean everything has been put back? All of that tatty old furniture gone?"

The detective and his police officers marched out of the house. The detective was in such a rush to get back to the Palace to see for himself that he tripped over Chipolata, who had sat himself in the doorway.

"Pigs! Disgusting!" said the detective.

Chipolata took offence and started sniffing around the detective's pockets. He managed to nudge out the address book. The detective got to his feet and ran out of the house without noticing the little book in Chipolata's mouth.

Everyone cheered.

Polly and Charlie cheered because they wouldn't be arrested after all. Gran and Mum cheered because they had put the room back to normal just in time. Rosa cheered because she had discovered her witch powers at last. She could do Instructions!

"Was that clever or what?" she said, whisking Chipolata off his trotters and giving him a huge hug. "That can be my own special Instruction – the room-transferring spell. Making that vacuum cleaner fly will be a doddle now!"

"You'll be able to come with us to the Meeting tonight," said Mrs Bollygum.

Rosa shrieked with delight.

Then it was Charlie who saw the problem.

"The wooden pig has gone," he said. "If you needed that for the Instruction how do you know you'll be able to do them without it?"

Rosa was shocked. She hadn't thought of that.

"What am I going to do?" she wailed. "I need that pig!"

"Don't be ridiculous!" Gran was saying. "You've got a pig. Chipolata! He's the only assistant you'll need. Ask any witch."

"But I couldn't do Instructions before," Rosa said. "It was the wooden pig. I can't do it without it."

Chipolata wriggled. His eyes stared straight into Rosa's and he gently nudged at her cheek with his pink nose.

"Chipolata is the one who is magic," Charlie said.

"It's all in your head," Gran said. "Tell yourself you can do something and you will!"

Rosa's mum agreed.

"You're a witch, Rosa," she said. "You are meant to fly and do spells. You don't need any magic trophies."

"Coo-ee!" there was a familiar voice at the front door. It was Charlie's and Polly's mum again.

"Oh, no!" said Charlie as Mum walked straight into the Bollygums' front hall. The lounge door was open and she could see straight in.

"I saw two police cars outside," she said, "and

wondered if everything was okay. I hope you haven't been burgled or... "

She had seen the Bollygums' lounge – the worn carpet, the tatty furniture and scruffy wallpaper. Then she saw Rosa with Chipolata and turned pale.

"What... what's happened to the room? It looks different!"

Charlie and Polly stepped forward.

"They decided they didn't like it after all," said Polly.

"How do you get that... er... old-looking effect?" Charlie's mum asked.

Charlie took his mum's arm.

He needed to think quickly.

"Really clever, isn't it? Er... Mum... I think they're about to give the pigs their breakfast. We should go."

That evening the great news of the mysterious return of the Queen's Lounge was on the news. Mum had a headache. When she had a headache she never watched TV. So, fortunately, she didn't see the new pictures of the Queen's room.

"They need to improve security at that Palace," Dad said. "First it's stolen and then it's put back and no one sees anything. It must have been magic!"

That evening, Charlie and Polly wished they could have gone next door to see Rosa leaving for the Annual Witches' Meeting. But they had to watch from Charlie's bedroom window instead. They couldn't risk the grown-ups asking any awkward questions.

Rosa's gran and mum had been right. Rosa didn't need the wooden pig. With Chipolata safely on her lap, she took off from the back lawn as though she had been flying vacuum cleaners all her life. Charlie and Polly waved from the window. The three witches must have known because they turned and waved back.

"See you tomorrow," Charlie said, even though Rosa couldn't have heard him.

Tomorrow would be Rosa's first day at Polly's and Charlie's school. Charlie felt a panicky shiver run through him. The thought of keeping the Bollygums' family secret from everyone at school was scary. He and Polly would be the only ones who knew the new girl in Year Four wasn't just any new girl.

She was really a witch called Rosa!

Hilary Hawkes Books

When Jason woke one morning to find he was beginning to disappear… well that was just the beginning of his problems that day!

Will anyone believe him?

Would his sister's school football team ever win a match?

Could Jason manage to rescue his friend George from the clutches of the crazy Dr Brillbot?

Available from bookshops or
www.robinswoodpress.com

Illustrated by
Mary Hall

ISBN 1-869981-820

Robinswood Press